The Merchant of Venice

Sweet Cherry

Publishing

Published by Sweet Cherry Publishing
53 St. Stephens Road, Leicester, LE2
1GH, United Kingdom

© Macaw Books
The Merchant of Venice

Text & Illustration by Macaw Books
ISBN-978-1-78226-015-8

Printed and Bound by CPI Group (UK) Ltd., Croydon, CR0 4YY

❦ About ❧
Shakespeare

William Shakespeare, regarded as the greatest writer in the English language, was born in Stratford-upon-Avon in Warwickshire, England (around 23 April 1564). He was the third of eight children born to John and Mary Shakespeare.

Shakespeare was a poet, playwright and dramatist. He is often known as England's national poet and the 'Bard of Avon'. Thirty-eight plays, one hundred and fifty-four sonnets, two long narrative poems and several other poems are attributed to him. Shakespeare's plays have been translated into every major existent language and are performed more often than those of any other playwright.

Shylock: He is a Jewish moneylender. He is shrewd and cunning, and disliked by everyone. He devises a clever plan to take his revenge on Antonio by demanding a pound of Antonio's flesh if he is unable to pay back the borrowed money on time.

Antonio: He is a trader and also a moneylender. He signs a contract with Shylock because of his love for his friend Bassanio. He is liked by everyone, unlike Shylock.

Bassanio: He is a gentleman and a friend of Antonio. He borrows money from Shylock through

Antonio. Though Bassanio later comes to his friend Antonio's rescue, he proves not to be much help.

Portia: She is a wealthy lady and the wife of Bassanio. Disguised as a young male lawyer, she tricks Shylock into forgiving Antonio even when he has no intention of doing so. She is beautiful, witty and intelligent.

The Merchant of Venice

Once upon a time in Venice, there lived a Jew called Shylock. Shylock was a moneylender. When people needed money, they would go to Shylock, and he would give them

whatever amount they asked for – but in return, he would not only fix a date and time when his money had to be paid back, but he would also charge them very high interest.

This led to most people in the city disliking Shylock. His biggest enemy, however, was a man called

Antonio, a noble trader. Antonio, like Shylock, would loan people money whenever they asked him for it, but in return, he did not chase them to repay him, nor did he charge his borrowers any interest. Thus, whenever Antonio encountered Shylock on the streets of Venice, he would leave no stone unturned in

insulting him. Shylock, being an evil, calculating man, never said anything to Antonio in return, but he was waiting for the perfect opportunity to humiliate and disgrace him.

Antonio was the kindest man ever known in Venice. Of his many friends, one was extremely

close to him. As a matter of fact, they were so close that they were more like brothers. But this nobleman, Bassanio, had one vice – he could never live off his income. His expenses were always wider than his pocket, and sooner or later he would always have to come to Antonio for money; not that Antonio minded.

One fine day, Bassanio arrived at Antonio's house and told him that he had found a way of restoring his fortune. He had fallen in love with a noble heiress called Portia. Bassanio knew Portia's father, and every time he had gone to their house, he had

seen her. Over time, they had fallen in love. But Portia's father had died recently, and Portia had inherited his fortune. Bassanio had decided that he was going to propose to her and ask for her hand in marriage. However, there was a problem. He wanted to wear

some fashionable new clothes for the occasion and, as usual, did not have any money. So he had come to borrow the sum of three thousand ducats from Antonio.

Antonio was overjoyed on hearing what Bassanio had to say. But at that moment he did not have much money with him. Some of his ships were to return from their voyages in a few days' time and then he would have enough money to lend to his

friend, but he knew the matter could not wait until then. So he decided to go to Shylock and borrow the money from him to give to Bassanio.

Bassanio was not happy with the idea, but Antonio insisted that there would be no problem, as his

ships were due to return soon. Once they reached Shylock and told him they needed to borrow some money, Shylock realised that it was the moment he had always been waiting for. He told Antonio that though he had always insulted him in public, Shylock had always wanted them to be

friends. Antonio was a little taken aback. Shylock went on to tell him that to show his good intent, he would not only lend Antonio the three thousand ducats, but would also not charge him any interest. All Antonio would have to do in return was go with him to a lawyer and sign a bond, which would

state that in the event Antonio
was unable to pay him back the

money within a certain amount of time, Shylock would take a pound of flesh from any part of Antonio's body he desired.

Bassanio was not very happy with this proposal and begged Antonio not to put himself in any danger because of him. But Antonio felt that he had

misjudged the Jew all along and
that his intentions were genuine,
so he immediately agreed to sign
the bond.

Finally, Shylock made the
required payment to Antonio.
With this money, Bassanio
obtained some fashionable clothes

for himself and, with another gentleman friend called Gratiano, left for Portia's house.

Within a few moments, Bassanio was able to get Portia to agree to his proposal. He told her that all he had was a noble name and birth, but not much money,

Portia told him in return that to be worthy of him, she would have to be a thousand times wealthier than she already was. Presenting a ring to Bassanio, she mentioned that all her wealth and her property, along with her own self, now belonged to him.

Meanwhile, Gratiano had fallen in love with one of Portia's

companions, Nerissa. As Portia and Bassanio were exchanging vows of love, Gratiano walked up to them and congratulated the happy couple. He then informed them that he too would like to get married. He explained that Nerissa would love to marry him, but only when Portia had married Bassanio. So Bassanio and Portia congratulated the happy couple, Gratiano and Nerissa.

While the two couples were merrily talking about their

fortunate affairs, a messenger arrived at Portia's house with extremely sorrowful news. All of Antonio's ships, which were

expected to arrive in a short while, had been lost at sea. The noble Antonio was now penniless.

Bassanio was completely shattered by this news. He told Portia how Antonio would always lend him money whenever he needed it, and also about the deal between

Antonio and the Jew. Seeing Bassanio turn pale at Antonio's message, Portia told him to make

haste to Venice and free Antonio from the bond immediately. She also insisted that Bassanio marry her, for then he would have a legal right over her money, which he could use to free Antonio.

So, a marriage was arranged with great haste, and Bassanio

and Gratiano were married to their beloved ladies. Shortly, both men set off for Venice. Upon arriving in the city, Bassanio was shocked to find that Antonio was in prison.

Although Bassanio immediately sought out Shylock to pay him the money and release Antonio, there was a legal problem in the whole affair. It turned out that even with all the gold in the world, Bassanio would not be able to help Antonio, for the legal bond clearly stated that in the event that Antonio was unable to pay the amount, Shylock would take a pound of flesh from any part of Antonio's body he wanted. So no one could save Antonio and

he would have to die. A day had been fixed to present the matter before the Duke of Venice, where it would be settled and the punishment given.

Meanwhile, Portia, who had sent her husband to Antonio's aid, knew that it was going to be very difficult for him to

release his friend from prison. She realised that to save him, she would have to do something herself. Without wasting any more time, she made haste for Venice.

Portia's father had a very close friend who was a counsellor in law. To this gentleman Portia wrote a letter explaining the matter. The lawyer sent his counsellor's robe, which she would have to wear in court, along with a letter, which explained what she should do in order to save Antonio.

So finally, Portia arrived at the court at the appointed time, dressed as a man in the counsellor's robe. She had also brought Nerissa with her, who was also dressed as a man and came as the counsellor's clerk.

They presented themselves before the

duke and handed him a letter from Portia's counsellor, stating that he could not make it that day because of an illness – instead, he had sent these young lawyers to fight the case on his behalf. And so the case began.

At first, Portia tried to reason with the evil Shylock. She begged him to show mercy and forget all

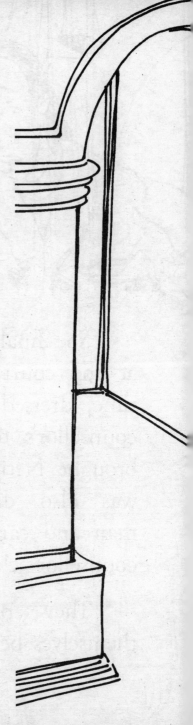

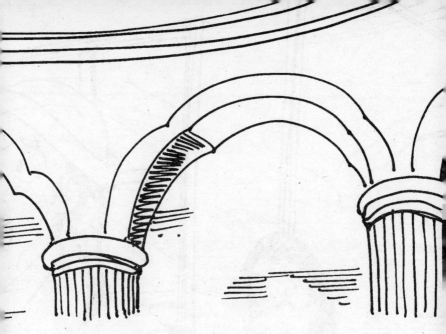

about the bond. She tried to tempt him by saying that mercy helps both the person granting it and the person to whom it is granted. But nothing could change Shylock's mind. He insisted that since it was written in the bond, he should be allowed to draw a pound of flesh from Antonio's body. That was all there was to it.

Bassanio also tried to put in a good word for Antonio, begging Shylock to reconsider his decision. He was willing to pay the entire sum to Shylock right at that moment, but Shylock clearly stated that he would not settle for anything but a pound of flesh,

41

because it was stated so in the legal agreement.

Portia then asked the court if at least a surgeon could be present when Shylock cut out a pound of flesh from Antonio's body. After all, Antonio could

bleed to death. But that was exactly what Shylock wanted. So he stated that since that clause was not in the bond, a surgeon could not be present when Shylock carried out his part of the deal.

Finally, Portia had no option but to agree to Shylock's proposal. She declared that the law indeed could not be bent and Shylock was entitled to demand his pound of flesh.

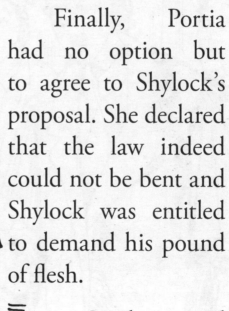

So she turned to Shylock and

said, "Take your pound of flesh, but without dropping a single drop of blood. And remember, you have to take a pound exactly, no less, no more."

Now Shylock was in a fix. How could he cut a piece of Antonio's body and yet there not be a drop of blood? And how on

earth could he be so accurate as to cut out exactly a pound of flesh? But Portia was now adamant that the bond stated that only a pound of flesh was to be taken and nothing more. And in the event that Shylock did not adhere to his part of the deal, she made it very clear that half of his property would go to Antonio and the

remaining half would be given to the state of Venice as a penalty.

There was no escape for Shylock now. He did not know what to do. He tried to say that he would be happy with his money, but Portia reminded him that the question of money was irrelevant, as Shylock himself had already stated.

Antonio said that he would be content if half of Shylock's wealth, which was to be handed over to him, went to Shylock's own daughter. Antonio knew that Shylock's daughter had married a Christian and so Shylock had excluded her from his will.

Shylock, unable to speak another word, claimed that he was ill and begged to leave. He told the court that they should draw up a contract and have it sent to him. He would then sign it at his house. So saying, the evil Jewish moneylender fled from the

court, outsmarted by the young lawyer.

The duke freed Antonio from bondage and even praised the young lawyer whose efforts had set Antonio free. He asked Bassanio and Antonio to make the payment of three thousand ducats to the young man. While Bassanio readily agreed, Portia did not and declined the offer of money. But when Bassanio took off his glove and revealed the ring that Portia had given him when they got married, the young lawyer promptly asked for it back, wanting to have some fun with Bassanio. Bassanio, who obviously did not know that the lawyer was none other than his wife, was reluctant to give the ring away.

But the lawyer would not take anything else

from Bassanio except the ring. Antonio then requested Bassanio give the ring away, saying, "Let him have the ring. Let my love and the great service that he has done for me be valued against your wife's displeasure." Bassanio obviously did not want to

dishonour his friend, so he gave the ring away.

Nerissa also played the game with Gratiano and took his ring as well. Both the ladies laughed as they left the courtroom, as they could now have some fun at their husbands' expense.

When they returned home, Portia and Nerissa changed into their usual attire and awaited the arrival of their husbands. Soon, Bassanio and Gratiano came back, along with Antonio. As Bassanio

was introducing Antonio to his wife, they heard a fight break out between Gratiano and Nerissa.

On being asked the reason for their argument, Nerissa told them that Gratiano had handed

over the ring to some clerk, a ring he had refused to part with when Nerissa gave it to him. Gratiano tried to explain why he had given the ring away and told the ladies the whole story.

But Portia, who also wanted to have some fun at Bassanio's

expense, reprimanded Gratiano and told him that he was still in the wrong for giving away the ring. Her husband would surely never do a thing like that, she said. But Gratiano, in order to shift the blame away from him, told Portia that Bassanio had first

given his ring away, and that was the only reason he had given his own ring away.

Portia appeared to be very angry upon hearing this. Bassanio tried to pacify her and told her the whole story again,

but she refused to listen to his explanation. Antonio lamented as to how he was the reason behind this feud. Had it not been for him, the married couples would not be warring like this. He then tried to calm Portia down by telling her that Bassanio would always

be true to her, and he himself would be the guarantor of that.

So Portia handed Antonio a ring and told him to give it to his friend, and to tell him that he should not give this one away to anyone again. Bassanio was amazed to see the ring, because it was the very one that he had given to the young lawyer. Only then did he realise that the counsellor of

law who had defended Antonio and saved his life was none other than his wife.

As the happy couples were rejoicing, a messenger came with the news that all of Antonio's ships which were presumed lost had come into the harbour. Antonio was once again a rich man!